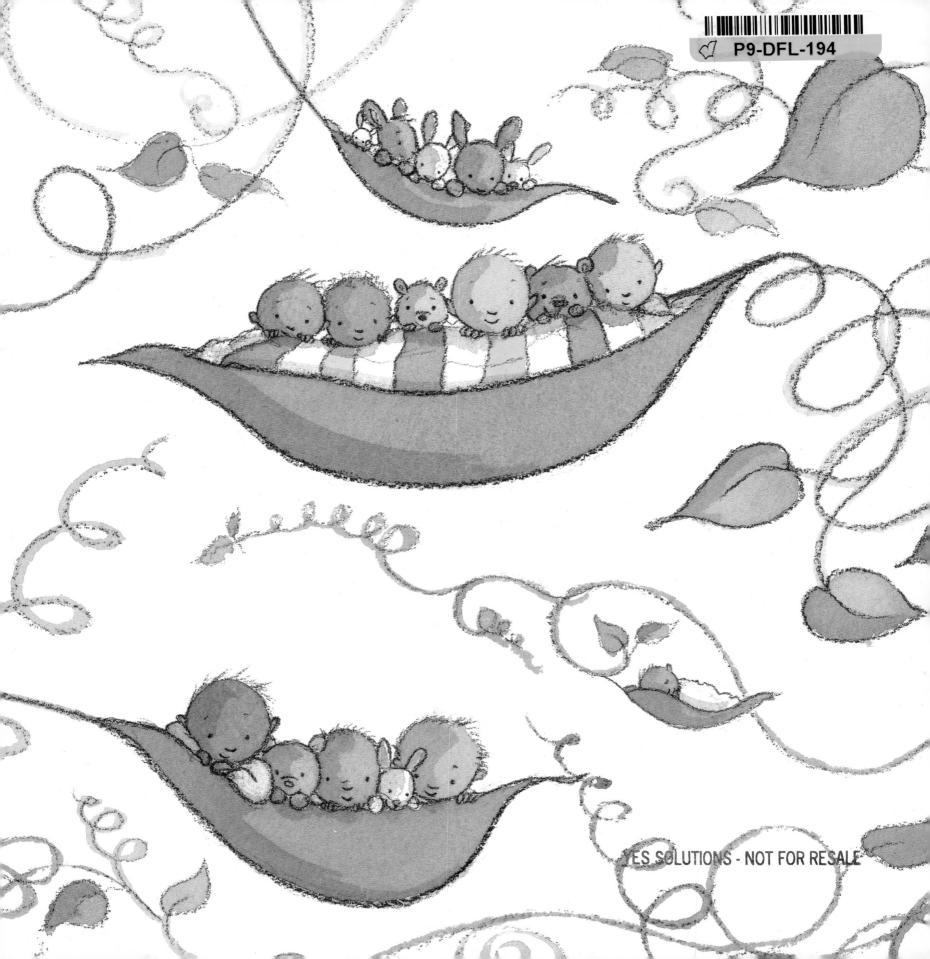

For Jake and Lucy
K.B.

For my American family Bernette, George and Olivia
S.W.

Text copyright © 2002 by Karen Baicker
Illustrations copyright © 2002 by Sam Williams
CIP Data is available

Published in the United States in 2002 by Handprint Books
413 Sixth Avenue
Brooklyn, New York 11215
www.handprintbooks.com

First Edition
Printed in China
ISBN: 1-929766-61-0
4 6 8 10 9 7 5 3

Tumble Me Tumbily

Written by

Karen Baicker

Illustrated by

Sam Williams

HANDPRINT BOOKS 🖐 BROOKLYN, NEW YORK

Part 1

Tumble Me Tumbily

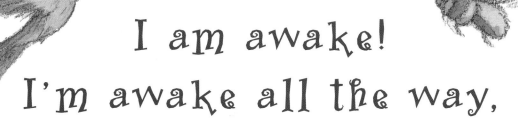

I am awake!
I'm awake all the way,

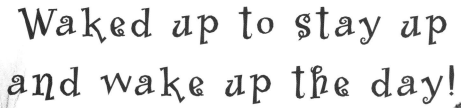

Waked up to stay up
and wake up the day!

Time to get Mommy
still sound asleep,

Butterfly kisses
to tickle your cheek.

Open the curtains
and let in the light,

Piggyback, off we go
holding you tight.

Bumpity-bump
as
we
go
down
the
stairs

Bidee-boom
bidee-bumbly

Bouncity bears.

Tickle me

tackle me

Sack-a-potato me,

tug-a-bug
jumble-bee

tumble me tumbily!

Catch me up

swing me up

in your

trapeze,

Hoppity
Pony ride
Bounce on your knees,

Slip-a-dip

Oops-a-daisy
Gallop-a-trot,

Hide
and seek

Here
I come

**Ready
or
not!**

Part 2
Yum Tummy Tickly

Tickle in my tum tum
time for tasty yum yum,
One bite for mommy
and one bite for me.

Flying spoonful
taking off
soaring in your hand,
Airplane riding
swooping gliding
coming in to land.

Grape jelly
jiggle belly
coming down the slide,
Smash a berry
messy, merry
mix it up inside.

Toot Toot!
Choo-choo
Coming down
the track,
Pretzel, cracker
tummy packer
bringing me my snack.

Smackily
we chomp and chew,
Open wide
and I'll feed you,
Another bite for mommy
and another bite for me.

Yum tummy tickly
pumpkin pumpernickly,
Whistling a noodle tune,
Making music
with my spoon.

Giggle greens and silly beans

jump up to the sky,

Dance and tumble,

apple crumble, fill-my-belly pie.

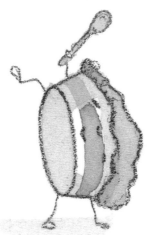

Empty dish
and sippy cup,
Wash my face
and pick me up.

No more bites
for mommy,
and no more bites
for me.

Part 3
Snuggle Me Snuggly

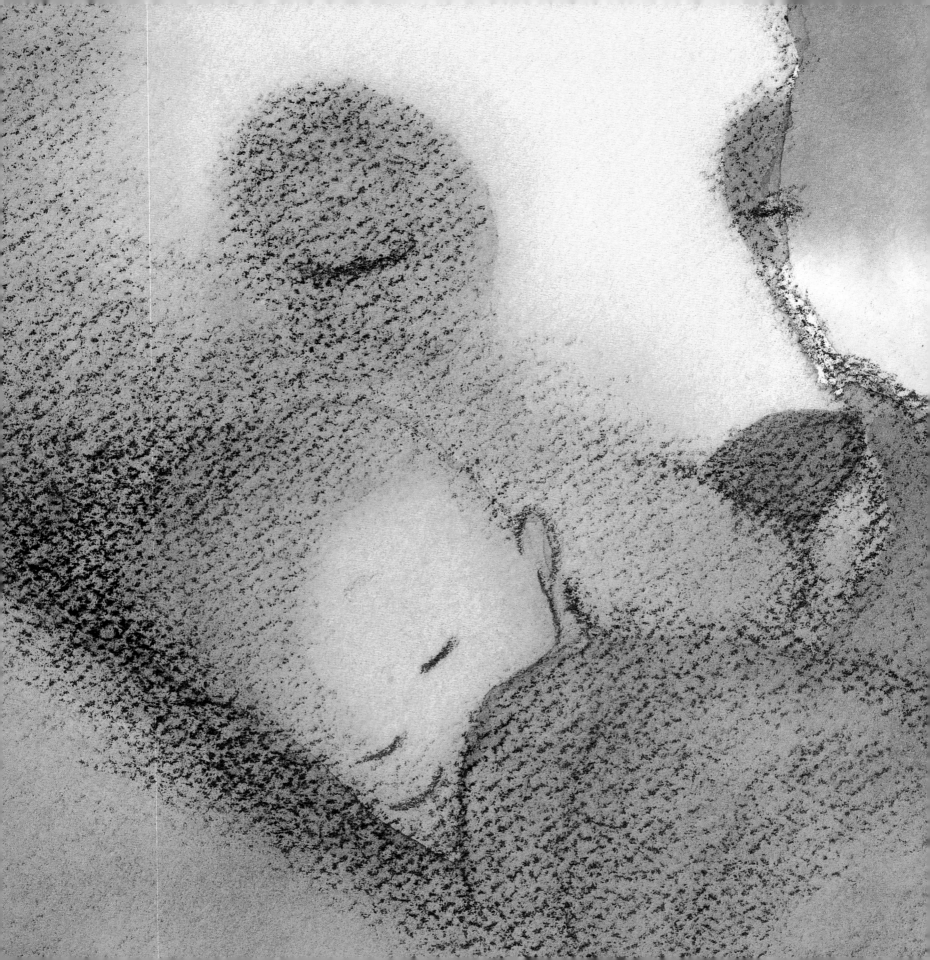

Snuggle me snuggly
so warm and cuddly,
Huggily, happily
in your soft lap I'll be,

Cuddly cozy
Eskimo nosy,
Silly and giggly,
closer than close
can be.

Nestled and nuzzly
cheek on your chest,

Bundled up baby bird
tucked in your nest.

Scoop me up

Swoop me up
off to the moon,

Love me up
hug me up
in your cocoon,

Sweetie pie
sleepy pie
sing me
a lullaby,

Hushabye
hushabee
come nighty-night with me.

Sweet peas
in pods are we
wrapped in your arms I'll be,

Dozily dreamily
rockabye honeybee,

Snug as a bug I'll be
with you so close to me,

Cozy my mommy
snuggle me snuggly.